Iraq: the country torn
apart by war and anarchy. And now,
terrorists have seized a Van Gogh
painting worth 25 million from one
of Saddam's palaces. The painting's
owner, a Kuwaiti prince, has asked
for Her Majesty's Government's help
in retrieving it. But rather than
agreeing to pay the terrorists'
ransom, ex-SAS hero Mick Kilbride
and his sidekick 'East End' Eddie are
sent undercover in a deniable
operation called Desert Claw. Their
brief is simple: retrieve the painting,
and eliminate the terrorists at the
earliest possible opportunity. The
mission sounds simple enough. But
as Mick and his team are drawn into
a dark and violent world, things are
not always as they seem. And in the
final climactic scene, a horrible and
shocking truth awaits the men.

DESERT CLAW

Damien Lewis

BBC
LARGE
PRINT

First published in 2006 by
Arrow Books
This Large Print edition published
2006 by BBC Audiobooks by
arrangement with The Random
House Book Group Ltd

ISBN 1 4056 2195 8
ISBN 13: 978 1 405 62195 3

British Library Cataloguing in Publication Data available

Printed and bound in Great Britain by
Antony Rowe Ltd., Chippenham, Wiltshire

This book is dedicated to the victims and survivors of the 7/7 terrorist attacks on London.
In particular my cousin,
Hannah Lewis.
Bowed but not broken.

CHAPTER ONE

'You go in hard. Very hard,' said the Major. He paused and eyed the four men in the room. 'You take down that building. You take out the enemy. And you seize that painting fast. I want it returned without a scratch on it. And one further thing. I want all the terrorists killed. All of them. Dead terrorists. No witnesses. No survivors. Is everyone clear?'

'Sort of,' Mick replied quietly.

Major Alexander Lloyd-Barrier. Mick had first run into him ten years earlier. Back then Mick had been a young soldier in the SAS. The Major had worked for some shadowy spying outfit. The Counter Terrorism Warfare Group, or some such name. Mick hadn't warmed to the Major back then and he liked him even less now. He leant back in his chair and tried to focus on the briefing.

'Mick, you're mission leader. You form a four-man fire team, together with Eddie, Jim and Jock.' The Major nodded at the three other men in the room. 'On arrival in Baghdad, you hook up with Summit Security. Mick, I understand you know Bill Berger, the director of Summit? He's been in Baghdad since the war. Runs a big security operation out there. He's got you eight extra men. That's two more fire teams. They're all British and American ex-special forces. Gives you a dozen men to do the job. Should be more than enough, don't you think?'

'Possibly,' said Mick. 'Yep. I s'pose it is.'

'Show a little enthusiasm, won't you, Mick?' said the Major. 'Oh yes, I almost forgot. The codename for your mission is Desert Claw. I repeat, Desert Claw.'

'It's been used before,' said Mick.

'What?' said the Major.

'Used before,' Mick said. 'Years ago, by the Yanks. That fucked-up mission in Iran, to lift the embassy siege.'

'You think I give a damn?' the Major snapped. 'As I said the codename for your mission is Desert Claw.'

'Hope it goes better than the Yank mission did, then,' Mick said.

Five years ago Mick had left the SAS, after fifteen years in the Regiment. Since then he'd worked as a photographer in his native Manchester. Outside of the military, photography was his main passion in life. But he hadn't made much money at it. So he'd agreed to be kept 'in reserve' as an old SAS hand to be called in when certain missions were required. The so-called 'black operations'. High risk. High danger. Top secret. And highly paid. Like now, with this crazy mission to rescue some dodgy painting in Iraq.

The meeting with the Major was

being held in Hereford, but not at the regular SAS base. The Major had rented a room in some cheap hotel. It seemed a bit odd to Mick. But he presumed it was all part of the 'black' nature of the mission. Keeping it all unofficial and away from British Government territory.

Mick glanced around the small, shabby hotel room. Luckily, he had his old team with him. Perched on the bed was his right-hand man, 'East End' Eddie. An old SAS hand, Eddie came from the rough end of London. He was hard as nails and sharp as a pin. Next to him was 'Kiwi' Jim, a veteran of the New Zealand SAS. A real joker and a good, honest soldier. On the far side was Matt 'Jock' McLane, a massive Scot. Also ex-SAS, Matt was a man of few words and a fearless warrior.

Like Mick, Jock, Kiwi and Eddie were all 'reserves'. They were Mick's A-team. They'd been on several black missions together. Without his

A-team behind him, Mick would never have considered the present mission. He turned back to face the Major.

'There's one thing that doesn't make sense, though,' said Mick. 'You're saying we fight our way into the building and kill all the occupants. It's going to be pretty bloody violent in there. So how do we do all that without damaging the bloody painting?'

'Mickey's got an effing point,' Eddie remarked. 'Might be a bit terminal, innit? I mean bullets and grenades on canvas ain't a medium I've 'eard of before.'

'We've thought of all that,' the Major snapped, ignoring Eddie's joke. 'On arrival in Baghdad you'll pick up several canisters of Sarin. Sarin as you know is a nerve gas. It is lethal to humans. It has no adverse effects on a painting, of course. You will be wearing full assault gear when you attack. Including gas masks. The terrorists will not.'

'Effing nice one,' said Eddie. 'So, we're gassing the bastards?'

'Not exactly Geneva Convention stuff, is it?' said Kiwi, quietly. 'Sort of thing Saddam Hussein got banged up for.'

'You're not being asked to do this because you're the Red Cross,' the Major sneered. 'You're being asked because you're ex-SAS. And you're being paid 300,000 dollars each for your troubles; 150,000 dollars up front. The rest on delivery. Perhaps the money will square your consciences? Plus the fact that they're terrorist scum. They need eliminating. And as I've made clear, this is a totally black operation. As far as Her Majesty's Government is concerned we've never heard of you. Or your mission. It isn't happening. You were never there. So any use of Sarin is nothing to do with us. Do I make myself clear?'

'Clear as mud, mate,' said Kiwi

Jim.

'We're flying British Airways are we?' Mick asked, changing the subject.

'Of course,' said the Major. 'As usual, you go out on BA in civvies. Low profile. Why?'

'Just wondering how we get the painting back home again. You do want it brought back, don't you?'

'I don't see the problem,' said the Major.

'Well, it's not every day you fly BA with a dodgy painting in your hand luggage, is it?'

'Does it matter? I usually fly first class. You don't have too many questions asked when you do. You never know. A few more missions like this and you might be able to afford to do so too. Anyway, you're clever boys. You'll think of a way to get it out, I'm sure.'

'Mind if we know the artist?' the Kiwi asked. 'I mean, we're risking our lives for a picture. Be nice to know who painted it.'

'I've no idea,' said the Major. 'It's not my department, I'm afraid. What I do know is that it's not especially valuable.'

'So, you don't know who painted it,' said Kiwi slowly. 'But you do know it ain't worth much. Right. Mate, I reckon that makes sense to someone, somewhere. Just not to me.'

'If it ain't worth nowt why're us blokes risking our necks to rescue it?' Mick added. 'And why does HMG want it so badly?'

'Yeah,' Kiwi added. 'Bad enough to pay us a whack of dollar to go get it?'

'Sorry,' the Major snapped. 'That's beyond what I can tell you. It's not your need-to-know.'

'Bugger that,' Mick replied. 'We ain't signed up for this one yet. And I ain't doing nowt unless I know why I'm doing it.'

'Me neither, mate,' Kiwi added.

'Jack shit'll happen,' Eddie confirmed.

'I'm with Mickey,' Jock growled.

'All right,' said the Major. 'This much I will tell you. And it had better be enough. The painting was once owned by a Kuwaiti prince. In the First Gulf War Saddam's forces invaded Kuwait and stole it. In the recent conflict, Saddam's palaces were looted. So the painting fell into the hands of this gang of Iraqi terrorists. Hence your mission.'

'If it ain't worth nowt why not just pay 'em for it?' said Mick. 'Why send us in?'

'It's not that simple,' the Major replied. 'The terrorists know it was originally looted from Kuwait. They think it's worth a fortune and are trying to sell it for one. They're mistaken, of course. Plus, we absolutely do not trust them.'

'It still don't make no effing sense,' said Eddie. 'I mean, if it ain't worth fuck-all, why're we bothering with it?'

'Look, the Kuwaiti prince wants it back,' said the Major. 'It's of emotional value to him, all right? He purchased it as a wedding present for his wife. HMG has agreed to help him get it back. It's a sort of quiet "thank you" for Kuwait's support in the recent war. We used Kuwaiti bases to launch the invasion of Iraq, you know.'

'Sounds like bullshit to me, mate,' Kiwi growled.

'Well, it isn't,' the Major snapped. 'And it's as much as I'm able to tell you. So, like it or lump it.'

'Total bloody bullshit, I reckon—'

'All right, mate,' Mick remarked to Kiwi Jim. 'Drop it, mate. Leave it.'

Mick turned back to the Major.

'I just want to know one more thing, Major. Who's paying? I mean with the four of us, that's over a million dollars. Plus there's the guys in Iraq. So who's footing the bill?'

'As it happens, the Kuwaiti prince

is.'

'So, is HMG making a profit on the job?' Mick asked. 'It wouldn't be the first bloody time.'

'What if they are?' the Major replied. 'And what's it to you? Look, am I wasting my time here? Just let me know, will you? If you don't want the job there's plenty of others who do. Now I need an answer. If you want it, I've got a video to play you. It's filmed by the terrorists and shows the painting. There's Arabic voices in the background and we've had them translated. But there's no point in me showing you if you don't want the job, is there?'

*   *   *

An hour later Mick and his team were heading back down the M6 to London. They had taken the mission, of course. It had been the money that had finally swayed them. The video had shown the front and reverse of the painting. A bunch of yellow flowers in a blue vase. Or was it blue flowers in a yellow vase? Mick couldn't really remember. He'd never been one for flowers much. Probably why his first wife had left him. He hadn't thought a lot of the painting, either. But the video had given him a sense of its size. Which was useful when trying to work out how to get it back to the UK.

'Major Wank-A-Lot,' Mick growled, as he stared through the windscreen. His Land Rover Defender was ploughing through a rainstorm. He was concentrating hard on the driving. 'He's a cold, mercenary bastard if ever there was one.'

'Always get the best missions with you, don't we, mate?' Kiwi remarked from the back. 'Like this one, I reckon. A dodgy op to go and gas some poor bloody Iraqis.'

'Put a bloody cork in it, will you, Kiwi?' Mick replied. 'You don't have to be here. No one's forcing you. And you don't have to get paid three hundred grand, all right?'

'Effing money's all right,' Eddie added from the passenger seat. 'Three hundred grand in an offshore account. I'll be able to refit me boat and take the missus touring the Caribbean for a year. Just Major Wanker there is the worry. I don't trust that fucker one inch.'

'Me neither,' Mick agreed. 'Weird. He don't seem to give a damn how we get the picture back home again.'

'Don't you worry on that front, Mickey,' Eddie replied. 'I got a guy in London. Big into art, he is. Real gentleman thief, too. He's smuggled this sort of shit 'arfway to hell and back. He'll know a way.'

'Should've known you'd know some dodgy geezer,' Mick said. 'Show him a copy of the video. It'll give him a sense of the size of the thing. Bloody great frame on it too. Bit hard to get that in your luggage, ain't it? And try and see if he knows who the artist is while you're at it.'

CHAPTER TWO

Two days later Eddie ducked down the stairs into the Beaujolais wine bar in Covent Garden. It wasn't his neck of the woods really. Too many farts in suits with posh accents. He preferred the Dog and Trout back home in Essex. He glanced around the bar. Tony was sat at his usual table, a pint already in hand. Eddie made his way over to him.

Tony looked up from his beer. 'How are you, old boy?' He rose unsteadily to his feet and extended a hand. Eddie shook it and took a seat.

'Never been better, Tony mate.'

For years, Eddie's dad and Tony had been as thick as thieves. In fact, they had been art thieves together. But Eddie hadn't met his dad until his mid-twenties. He'd been abandoned at birth at a local hospital, then brought up by foster parents. He'd messed around at school and joined the Paras at sixteen; at twenty-two he was in the SAS. By the time Eddie finally met his dad he was dying. Alcohol had done for his liver. Eddie reckoned Tony was almost an alcoholic, too. He'd stay sober most mornings, but by lunchtime he'd have started hitting the beers.

As Tony ordered a round, Eddie scanned the room. No obvious faces jumped out at him. No one he recognised. No one was paying them any attention, and no one had followed him in either. He relaxed a little and made some small talk. As he did so he could see the excitement burning in Tony's eyes. Eddie had spoken to Tony over the phone that afternoon. He knew that he was itching to talk about the painting.

'All right, old boy,' Tony began,

dropping his voice to a mumble. He leaned forward and tucked his club tie into his belt. 'I've looked over the video you sent me. And you know what? I am excited. Bloody excited. Shocked. A little scared even. Have you any idea what this is?'

'Not an effing clue, mate. That's why I'm here seeing you, innit?'

'Well, if I'm not mistaken it's a Van Gogh. An original.'

'Never 'eard of him. Only van I ever 'eard of is a Transit.'

'Sooner or later you might begin to wish you hadn't,' Tony replied. 'It's far bigger than anything I've ever handled before. People get killed for a fraction of the value of this painting.'

'What's it worth, then?' Eddie asked excitedly.

'Well, the video starts with a pan across the front of the painting. I managed to pause the image. Luckily, I've got the complete guide to Van Gogh's work at home and there's little doubt which it is. It's *Vase with Irises Against a Yellow Background.*'

Tony produced a photocopy of a page from his Van Gogh guide. He passed it across to Eddie.

'Yeah. That's it. Bunch of flowers in a vase, mate.'

'See the signature?' Tony pointed to a black scrawl at the bottom left of the painting.

'V-I-N-C-E-N-T,' Eddie spelled out. 'Even I can read that.'

'Quite. That's how Van Gogh signed most of his works. Just his first name—Vincent.'

'So, what's the damage, Tony?' Eddie pressed.

'Patience, dear boy,' Tony replied, with a beery grin. 'After the view of the front, the video shows the reverse. There's an export certificate glued to the back. I made a note of it.'

Tony passed another piece of paper across the table to Eddie.

'Never was one for puzzles much,' Eddie said, ignoring the paper. 'Just tell me what it's worth, mate.'

'See that?' Tony continued. 'That's the unique export code that any valuable painting is given. I checked with some people I know. It's the right number for this painting. For *Vase with Irises Against a Yellow Background*. Very few people would know that number. And certainly not a bunch of Iraqi terrorists. That tells me it's genuine. That, and the look of the thing.'

'All right, mate. But what's it effing worth?'

'See the number below the export code? It reads "1982-25m/US". That's the key. It means it was sold in 1982 for twenty-five million dollars. And twenty-five million dollars back in 1982! That's over twenty years ago, Eddie. Its value now is anyone's guess.'

'Jesus effing Christ.' Eddie let out a low whistle. Like Tony, his eyes were burning with excitement now. He'd suspected something dodgy was going down with Major Wank-A-Lot. But never this dodgy.

'Listen, Eddie, no painting's worth getting killed over,' Tony said. 'No matter what it's worth.'

'I don't plan on gettin' killed,' Eddie growled. 'I intend to be doing the killin'.'

'I don't really want to know too much—'

'An' I ain't tellin' you, neither,' Eddie cut in. 'Less you know, less danger you're in.'

'So, why exactly did you want me to look at it?'

'Let's just say we're on a mission and someone wants us to steal it. And kill a lot of nasty fuckers in the process. And you, Tony, have been in this art business for donkey's. Nicking, faking, forging, confidence tricking. You've done the lot. What I need to know is this. How the hell do we get this thing out of Iraq on a normal BA flight? That's without getting rumbled. Got to be a way, ain't there?'

'Of course, dear boy. What size is it?' Tony asked. He glanced down at his notes. 'It measures ninety by seventy centimetres. Simple. You lose the frame. Take it apart until you're left with just the canvas. Then you sew it into the lining of, say, a combat jacket. Something you might be wearing on the flight anyway. Knowing BA's record on lost luggage, don't you dare put it in the hold.'

'It won't show up on the X-rays or nothin'?'

'Of course not, dear boy. That's the beauty of canvas. It's material, just like any other. It'll look like another layer of lining in your jacket, that's all.'

'There's one more thing, mate,' Eddie said, looking Tony in the eye. 'I don't like this effing mission one bit. I don't trust the bastard who put us up to it. 'E's a real nasty fucker. In fact, I reckon he might be setting us up. Specially after what you just told me about the effing Van what'sit.'

'You think he might be trying to rip you off? Pull a fast one? Is that it?' Tony replied. 'I thought as much. Well, I've come up with an idea how you might just stop him. Quite a clever one, too, even if I say so myself. Get a round in, Eddie, and I'll tell you more.'

CHAPTER THREE

'Here's to Desert Claw,' Mick announced. He raised his beer bottle and clinked it with Bill's.

'Desert Claw,' 'Bronco' Bill replied, with a wolfish grin.

It was a week after the Major's briefing. Mick and his team had arrived in Iraq earlier that day. They'd been met at Baghdad

International Airport by Bill and a team from Summit Security. It was a hot and stuffy evening now and the air in Bill's Baghdad villa was stagnant. But at least the villa was secure; as the HQ of Summit Security, it was like a fortress with armed guards placed at all times on the walls.

Mick had already met the eight men who were joining his mission. They were all good soldiers. Two were Brits, ex-Special Boat Service (SBS), the sister regiment to the SAS. Mick knew both men, Woody and Geoff, from previous joint SAS and SBS training operations. The SAS and SBS had a bitter rivalry over who was the best of the best. But here in Iraq, that rivalry was quickly forgotten. Out here they were all brothers in arms. On this mission they were one team. Each man would need to watch his mate's back. If not, the mission would fail. And if it did, few if any of them would make it out of Iraq alive.

The other six soldiers were all Americans. They were either from Delta Force or the SEALs, the two top US special forces units. Mick knew only one of the Americans, a SEAL operator named Guy. He and Guy had been on joint operations in the Balkans. Guy was a tough soldier and a solid team leader. Mick would put him in charge of one of the fire teams. As for the rest of the men Mick knew the reputation of Delta and SEAL operators. As soldiers, they were second to none. Well, apart from the SAS, Mick liked to tell himself.

'Listen, buddy, I've got a problem with the plan,' Bill announced. He cracked open two more beers and thrust one across the table at Mick. 'You wanna hear about it, buddy?'

Bill spoke in a slow, Texan drawl. But Mick knew that his mind was razor sharp. Bill was a living legend in the US military. Almost twice

Mick's age, he was a veteran of Vietnam. After 'Nam he had gone on to set up Delta Force, the US version of the SAS. He was a celebrated shot with a sniper rifle. And despite the years, he still put in a session in the gym each morning. The two men had met many years before, on operations in Colombia. They'd been on several military and private operations since. Now Bill was out of the US army and making a fortune running Summit Security. Mick respected him as a soldier and a close friend. More than that he saw him as something of a father figure.

'Major Wanker's plan, you mean?' said Mick. 'We've all got problems with the Major. Tell me about it.'

'OK. Way I see it, you can't drive in to target,' Bill continued. 'Least not the ways you're thinkin' of. I took a look over your Major Wanker's plan. Say, what is a goddamn "wanker" anyways?'

'Wanker? It's what you do in the

bathroom when the missus is off sex. You know, with a porn mag. Or in your case probably the latest copy of *Complete Guide to Rifles and Carbines.*'

'Is that right?' said Bill, grinning. 'Well, I wouldn't know too much about it. I'm such a great lover, buddy, the wife's never off sex.'

'Is that why she's planning on leaving you, mate?' Mick replied. 'Anyhow, what's your problem with the plan?'

'Well, Wanker's plan says you drive in to target using three BMWs, right? Unmarked cars. Looking like local vehicles. Your team all in Arab dress. That's fine until you reach the target, in Al Khabur town. That's way out on the Syrian border, buddy. An' let me tell ya, it's a shithole. No one goes there. Not by choice, anyways. Whatever you're drivin' you'll be noticed. Soon as you hit town. And that kinda blows your cover. Blows your element of surprise. If the target gets a hint of what you're doing they'll be long gone, buddy. And you guys'll be in trouble.'

'So, what d'you suggest, mate?'

'You leave Baghdad in the BMWs all right. But then I got me three Land Rovers at a depot north of here. Ex Brit military. Fine pieces of kit, they are. Knock the socks off of a goddamn Humvee, any day. They're fully armoured. And I got them rigged with GPMGs and 50-cal heavy machine-guns. I got GPS tracking systems in 'em too, and some shit-hot electronic security. Now, you link up with the Land Rovers at the depot. Then you move up to target through the open desert under cover of night. You lie up in hiding all the next day. Then you hit the target that evening, just after dusk. You drive back that same night, but using the main roads. No need for surprise any more, 'cause you've done your job. You're back in Baghdad by daybreak.

Mission accomplished.'

'What about the local sheikhs who control the desert round there?' Mick asked. 'They weren't too friendly last time I was in their neck of the woods. Searching for SCUD missiles we were. Back in the last Gulf War. They're sure to know we're on the move, ain't they?'

'Oh, they'll know, buddy. Sure they will. But I know those guys. I work with them. See, I pretty much pay their goddamn wages, mostly. Costs me a bundle of dollars each month, just to keep 'em on side. I've spoken to them about your mission already. We kinda agreed a deal. They don't see no evil nor hear no evil. Not unless I tell 'em to. They ain't gonna do nothing when you pass by.'

'Sounds like you got it covered.'

'I gotta tell you, buddy, there's another reason I'm suggesting it,' Bill added. He lowered his voice and leant closer to Mick. 'You leave Baghdad in the BMWs and that's good. Everyone'll think you're sticking to the original plan. Major Wanker's plan. It might be better that way.'

'What d'you mean, mate? Who's everyone?'

'I don't know, buddy. I just kinda heard some whispers is all.'

'Like what kind of whispers?'

'Like maybe your mission ain't all that safe. Like maybe it ain't all it seems. Like maybe you're being set up or somethin'. It's only whispers. If I knew more I'd tell ya, buddy. All I'm sayin' is, it might be better to change the plan. Do the unexpected. Fox 'em.'

'Mate, I tell you, we got our own worries, too,' Mick said. 'That Major Wanker—I don't trust the fucker. There's no loyalty there. Not to us. Not to the mission. Not to his country. But I ain't got a sniff of what he's really up to. That's if there is anything dodgy going down.'

'Buddy, right now Iraq is a

goddamn nightmare. It's the Wild West out there. It's anarchy. And it's awash with US dollars. It's like Grand Theft Auto gone crazy. You ever played that game? Well, difference is, here it's set in the streets of Iraq. An' people ain't just stealing cars. They're stealing fortunes, buddy. Hundreds of millions of dollars. People are making and losing fortunes overnight. Yanks. Brits. Iraqis. You name it, they're all getting rich. Or losing it all. And it's getting my people killed.'

'Like how?'

'Like a couple of Brits. And a handful of Yanks, too. Good boys, all of 'em. They kinda knew too much and were gonna blow the whistle on the bad guys. So they got wasted. You gotta believe me—it's murder out there. I know you boys are ex-SAS. I know you can handle yourselves. But this is different. This is evil. There ain't no rules. There ain't few people you can trust.'

'Thanks for warning me,' said Mick.

Both men took a swig on their beers.

'So what d'you reckon to when we hit the target, mate?' Mick asked. 'Is it going to be a shit fight or what?'

'Piece of cake, I reckon, buddy,' Bill replied. 'Man, you got some real evil stuff to hit them with. I seen them canisters. That's nerve gas, buddy. Ain't gonna be no one left standing after you hit them with that shit. Best make sure your gas masks kinda fit real tight though.'

Both men chuckled at Bill's joke.

'So where is all that gear?' Mick asked. 'The masks and suits and all that stuff?'

'Out the back there. Locked up in my armoury real secure. But your boys back home done you real proud, you know? They got the canisters marked up with Arabic writing 'n' all. Real realistic like.'

'Maybe it's just some local Iraqi stuff they had lying around,' Mick joked.

'Listen, buddy, if they'd found any Sarin in Iraq we'd all know about it by now. No way would Blair and Bush be using it on this job. No way, buddy. They'd be showing it off in front of the world's media. They'd be saying: "See, we was right all along. Saddam did have WMD." '

'Too right they would,' said Mick. 'Tell you what though. You just got me thinking, mate. Get this. Maybe there's no fucking painting at all. No Kuwaiti prince. No looted palaces. Maybe we go in there and waste a load of Iraqis with the Sarin. And maybe coalition forces get sent in to clean up the mess. We're long gone. But they find the empty gas canisters covered in Arabic writing. What conclusion are they going to reach? Looks like a bit of nasty fighting between rival terror gangs. Just one lot had Sarin and the other didn't. So there's the proof that Iraq had WMD all along.'

'Could be, buddy,' Bill mused. 'But it's too damn complicated for me. Why go to all that trouble? And expense? And there's you guys and us. All witnesses. Be a damn site easier just to dump a load of Sarin in the bottom of one of Iraq's lakes. Then there's a tip-off and the coalition discovers them. Looks like they've found the site where Saddam hid his nasty weapons. The media's all over it in a flash. An' Blair and Bush are smelling of roses again. No. If y'all are being set up, buddy, that ain't it.'

'S'pose so,' Mick said.

Mick took a pull on his beer. Bill was one of the 'old and bold'. A wise old warrior. There was nothing better than having him around, Mick reflected. Too bad he wasn't coming on the mission.

'There's another thing, buddy,' Bill added. 'The word from the local sheikhs is this. Them boys holding that painting—they ain't no goddamn terrorists. Sure, they're low life. Petty thieves and gangsters. But they just got lucky when they seized that painting. Or at least they thought they did. Word from the sheikhs is they're out of their depth with it now. An' they're shit scared. But they ain't no terrorists, that's for sure.'

'Then what the fuck have we been ordered to waste them for?' Mick asked. 'We've been told to wipe 'em out.'

'I dunno,' Bill replied. 'No idea. Makes no sense to me, either.'

The two men sat in silence for a while, thinking and drinking. Mick didn't like this last bit of news one bit. He had trouble using Sarin on anyone. He knew what happened when people were hit by nerve gas. It was a horrible, evil way to die. He could just about stomach using it on terrorists. The sort of men who beheaded innocent people with blunt carving knifes. And videoed the whole thing. They were sick murderers and they had it coming. But a bunch of petty thieves? Jesus! Mick himself had been a bit of a crim in his youth. He'd done his share of thieving. Then the SAS had licked him into shape.

'Tell you another thing, buddy,' said Bill, finally breaking the silence. 'I'm comin' with ya on this one. Don't think I ain't, 'cause I wouldn't miss it for the world.'

'Mate, you're running a big outfit here. You can't afford the time. And what happens if you get wasted out there?'

'Fuck that. I'm comin' with ya whether ya like it or not.'

'Mate, I'd bloody love to have you along,' Mick replied. 'Trouble is, I don't think it's right. You got enough to do back here—'

'Listen, buddy, I ain't just doing this out of friendship,' Bill cut in.

'Not just for old time's sake, either. There's other reasons too. Them sheikhs in the desert. I know them all personally. If there's any trouble, I can deal with it. Plus you'll need an Iraqi guide. And there's only one I can trust. Omar. It's a long story, but he's kinda my right hand man. I saved his brother from being shot by a trigger-happy US marine. So, way I figure it you kinda need me along.'

'Wicked, mate. Bloody wicked. Welcome to Desert Claw.' Mick leaned across and slapped his American buddy on the back. 'But you reckon your old bones can handle it, mate?'

'Listen, buddy,' Bill growled. 'A few grey hairs don't make no difference. I could still out fight and out fuck a goddamn pansy Brit like you. Don't you never forget it. An' one more thing. Don't you go forgetting your American flags on this one.'

'What? Why? What's wrong with

the good old Union Jack?'

'Well, see, a lot of our boys don't recognise anything but Uncle Sam's Stars-'n'-Stripes. If you wave your UJ at 'em they gonna think you're goddamn Iraqis. Or Jordanians. Or Syrians. Hell, they could even mistake you for North Koreans for all I know. They don't have a goddamn clue. Fresh out of the cornfields of Alabama, mostly. And they're standing at the checkpoint up ahead, chewing their chewing tobacco and with itchy trigger fingers on their M16s. So, ya haul your American flag out the window. "Relax, son," you say to 'em. "You're doin' a fine job. We're proud of ya. We're coalition forces comin' through." '

CHAPTER FOUR

The following morning Mick and the lads were all nursing bad heads. Mick had stayed behind at the villa all evening, catching up with Bill. And the lads had hit the town until the early hours. A lot of beer had been drunk. But there was still work to be done. They were leaving Baghdad the following morning. They broke the gear out of the armoury and began checking it over. Mick's fire team had the task of hitting the target with the Sarin. So they had to remind themselves how to use the stuff. They fitted their gas masks with new filters then checked that the masks, suits and gloves all fitted perfectly.

Midway through the morning Mick sent one of the Iraqi guards into town. They'd forgotten a vital piece of gear: razor blades. Normally, the men never shaved on operations and growing a beard helped them blend in with the locals. But this time each man would have to be freshly shaven just prior to the attack. Any amount of stubble could prove fatal. It would stop the gas mask from making a proper seal with the skin, which would allow the deadly Sarin gas to seep inside the operator's mask.

Mick set about making up the explosive charges that he'd need for the assault. He paced out six feet on the villa floor. This was the average height of a door. Then he rolled out a length of blue, double-sided tape. When the protective strip was peeled away, it revealed a thick glue that would stick to just about anything. The side uppermost was just like a strip of normal gaffer tape. He ran a length of detonation wire down the centre of the tape and laid three lengths of black, sausage-like plastic explosive alongside it. Then he doubled them over, just to be sure.

He taped the whole thing up with gaffer tape. Then he rolled it up like a long black snake and shoved it into his backpack. If they needed to blow in any of the doors or windows, that's what they'd use.

Just as he'd finished making up the charges, Bill came over to check on things. He handed Mick a strip of white tablets.

'How's your head, buddy?' Bill said. 'Bad, huh? Well, don't go taking them pills 'cause they ain't aspirin, that's for sure.'

'What are they, mate?' Mick asked.

'NAPS tablets,' Bill replied. 'Sort of an antidote. Just in case you get some of that Sarin shit in your mask. Best start taking 'em now. That way you get a good dose in your system. There's enough for the rest of your boys, too.'

Mick glanced around at the other lads in his team. He'd heard all the horror stories about the NAPS tablets. The word NAPS is short for Nerve Agent Pre-treatment Set. British soldiers had been given these tablets during the first Gulf War. They were now being blamed for Gulf War Syndrome, the mystery illness that many Gulf War veterans have suffered from ever since.

'Bottoms up,' said Eddie, with a shrug of his shoulders. He threw the tablets into the back of his throat and took a gulp of water. That decided it for Mick and the rest of the team, who followed suit.

'Figure you might need these, too,' Bill added. He handed Mick a couple of US army injection sets. They contained needles and drugs. 'Take it you know what they are, buddy? Those are shots of atropine.' He pointed at two glass bottles of liquid. 'Guess you know how to use 'em, eh?'

'No worries, mate,' Mick replied. 'Just hope to hell we won't be needing them.'

Mick was a trained SAS medic. He knew what the atropine was for. It was the only known antidote for nerve poisons like Sarin.

After taking the NAPS tablets, Mick and his team began to feel sick and feverish. They were having a bad reaction to the drug. But they had a load more work to do, before leaving the following morning. Bill had built a short firing range at the back of the villa. Mick and the lads needed to zero in their weapons. Each man chose an MP5 sub-machine-gun as his main weapon. Plus a SIG-Sauer pistol as a back-up. All the weapons were fitted with silencers. And the Sarin canisters were designed to make almost no noise when set off. If everything went to plan, it would be a very silent, secretive operation. Mick hoped they would be in and out of the target building almost without anyone noticing.

They planned to leave all of their heavy weaponry with the Land

Rovers. The GPMGs and 50-cal heavy machine-guns, plus their light anti-armour weapons (LAWs) 66 m.m. rockets. If the mission went pear-shaped the plan was to head back to the vehicles. Then make their getaway into the desert. It would be hardest for the terrorists to follow them across rough country. And if they were pursued, they'd be able to unleash the big guns.

CHAPTER FIVE

Mick glanced at his watch. It was 6.00 p.m. Two hours until the attack. Just as Bill had predicted, the drive across the desert had gone like clockwork. The Land Rovers were tough, powerful workhorses. Whether it was ploughing through desert sands or fording dry riverbeds, they had been unstoppable. For the last twelve hours they'd been lain up in a desert wadi. The vehicles were covered in camo netting, the men resting in the shade. But now Mick could feel the adrenaline of the coming attack kicking into his veins. It was time to start getting the men ready.

'OK, final mission briefing,' Mick remarked quietly.

Eddie passed the word along. Soon all the men were gathered together for a heads up. Mick glanced around at his team. There were the eleven special forces soldiers, plus Mick. Then there was Omar the Iraqi translator, and big Bronco Bill. Fourteen of them in all. Mick couldn't have wished for a better team. He grabbed a stick and started sketching a diagram of the target in the sand.

'All right, I know we've been through this a dozen times,' Mick began. 'But, fail to plan and plan to fail. So, listen up. Here it is, one last time. You all know your call signs and frequencies?'

Mick received a series of affirmatives from the men.

'Good. Now from here it's a mile overland across flat desert to the target building. We move out at last light, around 8.00 p.m. Fire Team One, that's my unit, lead. Fire Team Two, that's Bill's lot, follow. Fire Team Three, that's you Guy, your lot take up the rear. Keep well spaced apart, in case we meet any hostiles. As soon as we move out we're on silent routine. No talking or radio use unless it's an emergency. Keep to the low ground, any cover and the shadows. We'll move tactically, so it'll be slow progress. We'll advance, take cover, watch out for the enemy, then advance again. I reckon we'll take an hour to reach the target. That means we'll be there by around 9.00 p.m. By which time it'll be pitch dark. Got it?'

'Got it,' the men replied.

'Right—the assault,' Mick

continued. He pointed at his diagram in the sand. 'This here's the target building. It's crucial we reach it without being detected. Surprise is everything. Our latest intel says there's no sentries on the outside of the building. But don't count on it. Inside, expect anything from ten to twenty hostiles. We expect them to be alert. We expect there to be guards. The painting is reported to be on floor three, here.' Mick pointed at the top floor of his diagram. 'That makes sense, as it's the most secure place to keep it.'

'Now, all three fire teams advance to this point, here. It's a patch of bush about thirty yards short of the target. Once there, we all take cover and wait out. We wait for as long as we need to properly observe the target. If we see any movement, anything suspicious, we stop and reassess the plan. If not, we go ahead. First, Fire Team Three, you get in position to cut the power lines.

OK? Once you're ready, you signal us. The signal is three flashes with your infrared torch. OK? Fire Team One then heads for the front of the building. And Fire Team Two heads for the rear. Once in position we radio we're ready. As soon as all Fire Teams have done so it's game on. Fire Team Three, you then cut the power. As the building goes black, that's the signal for us to attack. OK?'

The men nodded their confirmation at Mick. After what Bill had said back at the villa, Mick had a problem using the Sarin. If the Iraqis weren't terrorists it was wrong to go gassing them. But he'd made a decision not to share his concerns with the lads. And it was too late to reconsider now. Or to show a moment's hesitation. The mission was going down and that was that. Mick thrust his worries to the back of his mind. What the lads needed from him was leadership. Firm, rock-solid, fearless leadership. And that was what he was going to give them.

'As soon as Fire Team Three cuts the electric, it's going to go very dark in there,' said Mick. 'Hopefully, the enemy will think it's just a power failure. The moment it goes dark we get the Sarin in through the windows. We then wait twenty seconds. Should be long enough for the gas to start taking effect. Fire Team One then goes in through the front door and hits the stairs. As soon as we hit floor two we start gassing the rooms there. Fire Team Two, you hit the rear door and clear the ground floor. Fire Team Three, you keep both exits covered in case any enemy try to make a break for it. Got it?'

'Got it,' the men replied.

'Right. That's about it. We clear the building. Seize the painting. And get the hell out of there. Remember, there's to be no survivors. As you clear the building, you make sure the enemy is dead. They fucking should be. Sarin doesn't take any prisoners. But don't take any chances. If any are still alive by the time we're done, you shoot them. All our weapons are silenced. And I want this to be over as quickly as possible. We got a long drive back to Baghdad afterwards. All right?'

Mick looked around at his team and got a series of thumbs up.

'You all know the emergency plan, in case of a fuck-up. But there won't be one. We keep it simple, so nothing can go wrong. Any questions?'

'One thing, mate,' Eddie said. 'When do we suit up? Make like the Michelin Man? That's heavy gear. We don't want to be struggling with it when we're on top of the target.'

'Good point,' said Mick. 'We leave here fully suited up. Only thing you leave off is your gloves and gas mask. We'll put those on just before we hit the building. OK?'

Mick glanced around at the faces before him. The men were serious now. Psyching themselves up for the coming attack. They exuded the confidence of highly trained special forces soldiers. The atmosphere was one of an icy, killer calm.

Mick glanced at his watch. It was 6.45 p.m. 'OK. We've got ninety minutes. Let's make use of them. Check your weapons. Your explosive charges. And your protective gear. I want each man going in with at least five hundred rounds. Just in case of any real trouble.'

'And one last thing,' Mick added. 'I hope you all had a good shave this morning!'

There was a ripple of laughter. Then the men turned to begin their battle preparations. Mick paired off with Eddie. Together, they began punching rounds into fresh magazines. They were silent for a while, as they contemplated the coming mission. But Mick couldn't get the worries out of his mind about using the Sarin. Finally, he broke the silence. He figured he knew Eddie well enough to tell him what was eating him.

'Bill told me something back at the villa, mate,' Mick said. 'Been troubling me ever since.'

'What?' Eddie asked.

'The Iraqis in that building. Well, they ain't terrorists. Just petty criminals and stuff. I got no trouble gassing terrorists. But a bunch of muggers and car thieves? Bit bloody evil, ain't it, mate?'

'Is it?' said Eddie. 'Let me tell you somethin'. Last month my gran was mugged. She's seventy-eight. Bloke broke into her flat, banged her on the 'ead. Stole all her jewels. All to feed his heroin habit. She's in a home now and can't look after herself no more. If I had the chance to gas that bastard, you think I'd hesitate? Instead, he got six months inside. 'Nuff said?'

'Yeah, all right, mate,' Mick replied. 'Enough said.'

CHAPTER SIX

From the cover of the bushes Mick stared at the target building with unblinking eyes. It was barely thirty yards away. Their approach across the desert had been slow but sure. No one had noticed their passing. In spite of the chill desert night, it was hot and sticky inside the bulky suit and he could feel the drops of sweat trickling down his neck. He wiped the eye-piece of his night vision unit. Four windows were lit up in the target building. Every now and then he could see a figure flit across one of them. People were awake and active in there. But that was as he had expected. Everything seemed normal.

Mick scanned the building's perimeter. To one side there were a couple of pick-up trucks parked up. But they were deserted. He moved his night vision unit up to inspect the top of the building. It had a flat roof. That was one thing he hadn't been briefed on. If it had a flat roof there could be men up there. Guards. It was the obvious place from where to keep watch. He scanned the top of the building carefully. The eerie green glow of the night vision unit showed up the flat roof clearly. For a full minute he kept his eyes on that part of the target. But there was no movement. It looked deserted up there.

Above the flat roof it was a brilliant, starry night. There was far too much moonlight for Mick's liking. But there was fuck all he could do about that. It was time to start the attack.

Silently, he signalled for Fire Team Three to advance to the power line. With his heart in his mouth, he watched their hunched figures flit through the darkness. Barely thirty seconds later there were three red flashes coming out of the night. They were signalling they were in position and ready. Mick thanked his lucky stars that Bill was on the team. Fire Team Three were using one of Bill's special gadgets to cut the power to the target. It would send a massive electric surge through the line into the building and blow all the fuses and light bulbs. Even if the terrorists had a back-up generator, it wouldn't be of any use, the whole electrical circuitry of the building would be fried.

Mick glanced across at Eddie, Kiwi Jim and Jock. He placed the palm of his hand on top of his head. It was a sign that meant 'on me'. Then he turned and headed towards the front of the building at a crouching run. His heart pounded in his head. If there was one moment when the mission was most likely to be blown, this was it. He rounded the corner and flattened himself against the wall. A split second later Eddie was at the opposite side of the window. Then Kiwi and Jock were on either side of the front door. Quick as a flash Mick whipped out a Sarin canister from his chest webbing. At the same time, Eddie unhooked an axe from his belt. Mick looked across at Kiwi and Jock. Kiwi gave him the thumbs up. They, too, were ready.

Mick glanced down at the Sarin canister. He grabbed the pin holding the retainer clip. It glinted in the light from the window. Once he pulled it the canister was primed to pump out its deadly gas cloud. This was the point of no return. Gently, he eased the pin free. Only his hand was holding the retainer clip now. Once he released his grip, the clip would fly free. Then there were five seconds before the gas would start pumping. He pressed the 'send' button on his personal radio. The radio pick-up was pressed against his neck. It was so sensitive it would transmit even the faintest voice message.

'Alpha One, ready,' Mick whispered into it.

'Alpha Two, ready,' came the whispered reply from Bill.

'Alpha Three, ready,' came Guy's reply.

A split second later there was a fizzing and a popping of light bulbs inside the house. Then the whole building went black. At exactly that moment Eddie swung the axe through the window. The noise of breaking glass was covered by Arabic cursing, as the men inside crashed about in the darkness.

Mick heaved the Sarin canister in through the broken window.

He began counting, silently, in his head. One. Two. Three . . . As he did so, he grabbed his gas mask off his belt and pulled it over his head. He covered the filter with his hand, and took a sharp intake of breath. It sucked the mask tight against his face, proving that it made an airtight seal. He pulled on his thick gloves and continued counting. Ten. Eleven. Twelve. He could hear a faint hissing from inside the building, as the canisters released their deadly gas. And then there was a gasping and choking from inside the room. Bodies smashed into furniture. Mick heard a man vomiting violently. Another thrashing about as he struggled to breathe. Another's strangled screams as the gas took hold.

For an instant Mick was struck by a terrible image of what it must be like in there. Darkness. Total confusion. Then the first gasp of the gas. A moment's terror and panic as each man tried to flee. And then the gas had got them. Burning down their windpipes and choking their lungs. Mick knew what nerve gas did to people. What a horrible death it was. He tried to blank the images from his mind. Images of writhing bodies. He tried to tell himself that they were terrorists. That they had it coming. But Bill's words kept ringing in his head: 'Sheikh says they're no terrorists, buddy . . . Just low-life thugs and petty thieves . . .'

Seventeen. Eighteen. Nineteen, Mick counted.

Twenty! Mick smashed his boot into the front door with all his strength and violence. The cheap wood splintered and then he was kicking his way into the dark interior. He had his MP5 machine-gun at the shoulder. The torch attached to the weapon swept the room with a beam of light. The air was thick with an oily, white gas that danced in the light of the beam. Bodies writhed in front of him, clawing at the floor. No one noticed him. No one cared. Their eyes were blinded by the searing gas. They were dying.

Mick jumped over a figure heaving and vomiting on the floor in front of him. Two quick strides and he was at the rear of the room. The stairs lay up ahead. Instantly, Eddie was at his shoulder. Kiwi and Jock were on the far side of the stairwell. Mick paused as he and Jock grabbed a Sarin canister each. They pulled the pin and held down the retainer clip.

Mick signalled to Eddie and Kiwi to hit the darkened stairs. The two men pounded up the wooden staircase, sweeping the area above with their weapons. Mick and Jock followed, right on their heels. They could have done this with their eyes closed. Back at Bill's villa they had memorised every detail of the building's layout. Two doors lay off the top of the staircase, one to the front and one to the rear. Mick let the retainer clip fly on the Sarin canister. And then Eddie hit the first door, his boot crashing into the wood. The second he did so Mick tossed the Sarin inside.

A ghostly figure appeared at the dark doorway, cursing in Arabic. He raised an AK47. But as he did so,

Eddie fired. Thwoop! Thwoop! Thwoop! Three silenced bullets at point-blank range from his MP5. For a split second the young Iraqi's eyes bulged outwards. Then his face caved in where Eddie had shot him. He keeled over and hit the floor. A horrible choking and gasping came from the room behind him. Mick knew that the gas would deal with the others.

Clearing floor three was their priority now. And getting their hands on that painting. It was up there somewhere. And Mick needed it intact and unharmed. The four men paused for a second at the bottom of the stairs. Mick and Jock grabbed a third Sarin canister. On Mick's signal they hurled them up the stairwell, into the hallway above. He didn't want any shooting up there and risk harming the painting. He was going to use Sarin overkill instead. He grabbed a fourth Sarin canister. Carefully, they crept up the stairs. At the top there was still no sign of the enemy. In a repeat of the attack on the floor below they hurled canisters into the rooms. But still there was no sign of anyone.

'I can't see a fuckin' thing with all the gas,' Eddie yelled.

'Got to search the place,' Mick yelled back.

Covering each other, Mick and Eddie moved through the front room. Kiwi Jim and Jock were doing the same at the rear. But still they could find no Iraqis. Then Mick heard a faint burst of static on his radio, which meant he was getting a call from one of his men.

'Mate, there's a stairway back here that goes up to the roof,' came Kiwi Jim's voice. 'Reckon you better come join us.'

Mick and Eddie hurried across to the back room. Kiwi Jim and Jock signalled them over to one corner. A flight of metal steps led up to the roof. A trapdoor in the ceiling was open. Through it Mick could see the starlit sky. Clearly, the metal steps would only take one man at a time. Mick glanced around at the other three men.

'Volunteers?' he asked with a grin.

'I'm right behind you, mate,' Kiwi Jim replied.

'Jock, you're an effing nutter,' said Eddie. 'You go.'

'Fook it,' Jock replied. 'A'right.'

Before Mick could stop him the big Scot put his foot on the steps and started climbing. As his head neared the top he switched off the torch beam on his MP5. He reckoned there was enough moonlight up there to see and kill by. The torch beam would simply make him an easy target. He brought the weapon to his shoulder. With one hand he held onto the steps and with the other he kept his gun aimed. As he crept up the last few steps, Kiwi Jim joined him below. As Jock's head emerged from the trapdoor on the roof he tried to stay as light on his feet as possible, already searching for the enemy.

He scanned the roof. There was not a lot of cover. A pile of wood to his left and an old bicycle leaning against it. Lines of washing right in front of him. Some oil drums off to the right. With just his head and shoulders above the roofline Jock kept scanning for the enemy. They had to be up here somewhere, he just knew it. For several seconds he stayed like that, silently listening out and watching. Finally, Jock placed one hand on the deck and vaulted onto the roof. As he rolled away from the trapdoor, he heard a crash. One of the oil drums had gone over. A moment later there was a deafening burst of gunfire.

Jock came to his feet in a crouch, his weapon at the aim. Bullets were tearing all around him and ricocheting off the roof. Instantly he sighted on the muzzle flash, just above the oil drums. He squeezed off three silent rounds. A double tap. Two to the body to drop him. One to the head to make sure he was dead. In this game it was about being first on the draw with accurate fire. The Iraqi's had been way off the mark.

Jock changed position now, then scanned all around him. Kiwi Jim vaulted out beside him. He was quickly followed by Mick and Eddie. Jock and Kiwi Jim took the right side of the roof, Mick and Eddie the left. As Jock advanced he kept his eyes on the oil drums up ahead. There were more of the enemy behind them, he just knew it. Suddenly, a figure broke cover and made a run for it. Instantly, Jock had him in his sights. It was a young Iraqi, no more than sixteen years old. He had an AK47 clutched in one hand.

'Drop the fucking gun, laddie,' Jock yelled. His words were muffled and distorted through the gas mask. 'Drop the gun!'

Within seconds, the young Iraqi was cornered on the edge of the roof. Jock advanced slowly towards him, keeping him covered as he did so. The Iraqi took a fearful step backwards. Jock's bulky suit, gloves and mask made him look twice as large as normal and he towered over the young man. The Iraqi jerked his head from Kiwi to Jock and back again. He took another step backwards, his AK47 dangling in his hand. The edge of the roof was now right behind him. He had nowhere to retreat to.

'Drop the gun!' Jock growled.

Suddenly, there was a horrible cry. The terrified Iraqi had taken another step backwards and disappeared from view. Jock took a quick stride to the edge of the roof and peered over. Spread-eagled below him was the young Iraqi's body. He'd fallen onto the back of one of the pick-ups parked below. He was lying perfectly still, but at an odd, unnatural angle.

It looked to Jock as if he had broken his neck. No doubt about it, he was dead.

'Thank fuck for that,' Jock muttered, as he turned away. The Major had ordered that they take no prisoners. At least it meant that Jock didn't have to shoot him.

'All clear on the roof, I reckon,' Kiwi announced via the radio net.

'You got it,' Mick replied.

'Let's go find the effing painting,' Eddie added.

Together with Kiwi Jim, Jock strode back across the roof to join Mick and Eddie. But as he did so he caught a shadowy shape out of the corner of his eye. There, hidden among the washing, an Iraqi was raising his weapon. They had missed one of the bastards. Jock swivelled with his gun and squeezed the trigger. But the noise of his silenced weapon was drowned out by the bark of the Iraqi's AK47. There was a flash of muzzle flame as the enemy fired off a wild burst. Then he keeled over, his weapon still firing on automatic. Jock followed him down with his gun sight. The Iraqi lay still on the roof, his body tangled in the washing. Jock could see a pool of blood staining the sheets a deep red.

As Jock allowed himself to relax a little he felt a sharp pain in his jaw. He must have been hit. He lifted his hand to check, but could feel nothing through his heavy gloves. He shone his torch beam on his glove. There was a small patch of blood. It couldn't be anything serious, Jock told himself. Most likely a flesh wound from one of the stray AK47 rounds. He'd deal with it later, once the mission was over. It had to be nearing its end.

Jock turned to the others and the four men headed back towards the trapdoor. As they hurried down Jock was the last to leave. He checked the roof one last time, just to be sure. Then he took a few steps down into the gas-filled interior. As he did so, the Sarin swirled around his knees. It was still thick like a fog in there. A second later the gas was over his head.

Suddenly, Jock took a choking, burning gasp. He felt his windpipe clamp shut, as he was hit by a wave of searing pain. He couldn't breathe! He couldn't breathe! He clutched in panic at his throat, unable to comprehend what was happening. Then the nausea swept over him. He collapsed and his body went crashing down the metal steps.

Jock landed in a heap on the floor. With the last of his energy he punched the send button of his radio. But he was incapable of speaking. All that came out was a choking, rasping series of gasps. 'Aaahhh . . . Aaahhh . . . Aaahhh . . .'

CHAPTER SEVEN

'What the fuck?!' said Mick, responding to Jock's radio cry. The noise had sounded ghostly and horrific. 'What the fuck was that?!'

Mick turned to check behind him. With a shock he caught sight of Jock slumped on the floor.

'FUCKING JOCK'S DOWN!' Mick yelled. 'JOCK'S DOWN!'

In one swift move he dived back to the foot of the metal steps. Eddie and Kiwi were right on his heels. Mick grabbed Jock and rolled him over on his back. His torch beam showed a slick of blood and shattered rubber at the big man's neck. And a scum of vomit on the inside of his gas mask. In a flash Mick realised what must have happened. *Jock had been hit in the face.* The round must have punctured his gas mask. He had been hit by the gas. He needed the Sarin antidote and fast.

Mick began scrabbling desperately in his chest pouch. The thick gloves made it all but impossible to find it. But suddenly he had the syringe in his hand. He raised it above his head and then plunged the big needle downwards. It penetrated Jock's thick suit and his combats. And then Mick punched the syringe of drugs into Jock's arm muscle.

Mick was small for an SAS soldier. But his body was as thick as a tree trunk and he was as strong as an ox. In one swift move he bent down and hauled the big Scot up onto his shoulders.

'Find the bloody painting!' Mick yelled to Eddie and Kiwi 'I've got to get him out of here.'

With that Mick turned and headed down the stairs. He was deeply worried about his big mate Jock. But he'd had only a few seconds exposure to the Sarin. Then Mick had got the antidote into him. It was crucial now to get him outside and into the fresh air. From his medical experience Mick reckoned that Jock stood a good chance. Or so he hoped.

He reached the bottom of the stairs where the room was still wreathed in gas. At Mick's feet there were figures twitching and convulsing in their death throes. Mick's torch beam probed the darkness. Everywhere his men were checking the enemy dead. The light caught in a slurry of vomit. An Iraqi body lay next to it. Mick could see that the Iraqi had shit and pissed himself too. The nerve gas had wrecked his bodily functions. The stench would have been sickening, but nothing made it through Mick's gas mask.

Mick hurried on. He ran right past Bill and charged through the back door of the building. He dumped Jock down on the ground. Then he grabbed the knife off his chest harness and sliced through the rubber straps on Jock's gas mask, then ripped the mask off his face. He used his glove to wipe the worst of the vomit away. Then he gave orders to Guy and the Team Three lads to patch up the flesh wound to Jock's jaw. As soon as Jock was able to drink, they were to get as much water down him as possible.

Mick turned and hurried back into the target building.

'What's up with big Jock, buddy?' Bill yelled.

'Took some Sarin,' Mick yelled back. 'Got the antidote into him. He'll be OK.'

Bill gave him a double thumbs up. Then he jabbed a gloved finger at his watch.

'Time we was leaving buddy!' Bill yelled into Mick's ear.

Mick nodded. 'Still checking the dead,' he yelled back. 'Plus searching for the painting.'

'You what?' Bill yelled. 'It ain't up

71

there?'

'It's got to be. Can't see much though. Gas like pea fucking soup up there.'

Mick glanced around the room. He started doing a body count. There were five dead in here. Maybe ten on this floor all together. Another twenty above. Thirty enemy dead and still counting. But the weird thing was how so few Iraqis were on the top floor. If that was where the painting was, why weren't there more men guarding it? Mick wondered. He was jerked out of his thoughts by the sudden arrival of Eddie at his side.

'There ain't no fucking painting!' Eddie yelled through his gas mask.

'What?!' Mick shouted back.

'No painting!' Eddie yelled. 'On the top floor. It ain't fucking here!'

'It fucking has to be!' Mick shouted back. 'What else were all these fuckers guarding?'

'Well it ain't! You want us to tear

the fucking place apart? We don't have the fucking time.'

'Listen, are there any of them fuckers left alive up there?' Mick asked.

'On floor two should be. They were hit last by the gas.'

'Right. Get me one. We've got some questions to ask him.'

Twenty seconds later Eddie came staggering back down the stairs. He had an Iraqi draped across his shoulders. A spare gas mask was clamped on the dying man's face. Eddie dumped the man at Mick's feet. The Iraqi was in a bad way. His trousers were soaked with urine. He foamed at the mouth and shook like an electric current was tearing through his veins.

But he was alive. Mick whipped a syringe out of his breast pouch and then held it up so that the dying man could see it. Then he grabbed Omar, their Iraqi guide, by the arm.

'Right, Omar. You tell him this is

the Sarin antidote,' Mick said. He held up the syringe of atropine. 'Tell him he gets an injection in exchange for the painting. If not, he'll be dead in three minutes.'

Omar knelt down and spoke into the Iraqi's ear. The man's body began to shake and twitch violently. He was gasping for breath. Saliva dribbled out of his mouth and nose. His eyes rolled and he spewed a stream of vomit into the front of the gas mask. Yet, somehow, the dying man managed to raise a shaking hand. He pointed to a section of the floor at Mick's feet and mouthed a couple of words in Arabic.

'Trapdoor. Under the carpet,' Omar said. 'It's in there.'

'Right, Eddie, give him the fucking antidote,' Mick ordered. He handed Eddie the needle.

For a second Eddie hesitated. Their orders had been to leave no man alive.

'Don't fuck around, mate!' Mick

yelled. 'We've got to keep him alive till we find the fucking painting.'

Eddie gave Mick the thumbs up, then plunged the needle into the Iraqi's arm. Mick turned and kicked back the carpet. His torch revealed a crude wooden trapdoor. There had to be a cellar beneath the floor. Mick heaved on the handle. But it was locked. From the inside. Which meant there had to be more of the enemy down there. Mick had no idea if they were alive or dead. But he wasn't taking any chances. Quick as he could he whipped out a shaped charge from his chest pouch. He peeled off the protective strip. Then he chose a spot on the floor several feet back from the trapdoor. He taped the charge to the floor in a crude square. Then stepped back to set the fuse.

'Listen,' he said to Eddie, Kiwi Jim and the others. 'I ain't blowing the trapdoor. That's the way they'll expect us to come in. Plus I might blow the painting. So I'm blowing a mouse hole through the floor. Soon as the charge goes we go in. Got it?'

The men nodded. They took several steps back as Mick set the fuse. Seconds later there was a sharp crack. A section of the floor had caved in and was now a smoking hole. Quickly Eddie lowered his powerful frame through the floor. He dropped, hit the deck, and crouched with his gun at the shoulder. He scanned the room with his torch beam. There were thick wisps of gas in the air. And three enemy, all face down on the floor. They looked pretty dead to Eddie.

Mick and Kiwi Jim dropped in next to him.

'Check them,' Mick yelled, pointing at the enemy with his gloved hand.

Eddie moved forward as Kiwi Jim covered him. Mick slid around the wall towards the rear of the cellar. At the back there was an old wardrobe.

He stuck out his gloved hand and grabbed the door handle. He pulled, but the door was locked. Fuck searching for the key, Mick told himself. He grabbed the door handle with both hands and yanked with all his might. With a tearing of wood the door came away from its hinges. Mick threw it to one side.

He shone his torch inside. There in the back of the wardrobe was a shapeless bundle. Whatever it was it was wrapped in an old curtain. Mick grabbed it and pulled it towards himself excitedly. Then he ripped down a corner of the curtain. The edge of a golden picture frame was glinting in the torchlight. Mick knew this had to be it. At last. They'd found it. The painting.

Behind him Eddie rolled over the third body, just to make sure he was dead. But as he did so, his torch glinted on something lying on the floor. Something round, metallic, about the size of an apple.

GRENADE! Eddie didn't need to check. He knew that the dying Iraqi had set a trap. He'd pulled the pin and then lain on the grenade, to booby-trap his own body. In a split second Eddie rolled the Iraqi back over. Then he slammed his own body down on top of him. As he did so, there was a massive explosion. He felt himself lifted off the floor and thrown clear of the corpse. And then his world went black.

Some time later Eddie came to, groggy and confused. The whole of the space in front of him was filled with smoke. He had lights shining in his eyes. And he could barely see. He tried wiping the circular glass eye-pieces of his gas mask. As he did so he glanced at his gloved hand and realised that it was covered in human gore. He glanced down at his suit. It was spattered with thick gouts of blood and flesh. He couldn't work out whose blood it was. His own? Or someone else's?

Then it all came back to him. The Iraqi corpse. The booby-trap. The explosion. Eddie looked up from his blood-spattered suit. Across the other side of the cellar Mick and Kiwi Jim were staring at Eddie as if he was a ghost or something.

'What? What are you fuckers staring at?' Eddie yelled. 'So I dived on the grenade. So what? It wasn't you I was worried about. It was the fucking painting!'

CHAPTER EIGHT

The convoy of Land Rovers sped along the dark road, wheels humming on the tarmac. Spaced well apart, fifty metres between each vehicle, they made less of an easy target for an ambush. They had been on the road for four hours now and the target building was many miles behind them. Mick's vehicle was in lead position and he had Bill at his side. Behind Bill was Omar. The painting was safely stowed in the rear. Big Jock was sitting next to it, recovering from his dose of Sarin gas. And Eddie was all bandaged up beside him. The dead Iraqi's body had taken the brunt of the grenade blast and Eddie had suffered nothing more than a few minor flesh wounds. And the painting had been left unharmed.

Bill's Land Rovers were fitted with the latest security gadgets. Most useful of all were the tracking devices. Powerful computers based in Bill's villa HQ kept track of the Land Rovers. An electronic map in the villa's operations room showed each vehicle's progress. And there was a hotline from the villa to the main US military commanders. Bill used it to keep a track on the US military checkpoints. All of them were marked on the electronic map. And if a location was changed,

Summit Security would be the first to know.

As the convoy ploughed ahead one of Bill's men was in constant radio contact with him. He was watching their progress on the map and then warning Bill of each US checkpoint up ahead. Anyone else on that road they would treat as potentially hostile. Several US checkpoints had already been passed in this way. At each, Bill had done the same routine. US flag out of the window. A grin and a 'You're doin' swell, boys. We're proud of ya.' Then a flash of his Summit Security credentials, and the convoy would be waved through. It was all going like clockwork, just like Bill had said it would.

Mick glanced at the luminous dial of his watch. It was 3.00 a.m. At this rate, they would be back in Baghdad by sun-up. He settled into the driver's seat and wrapped himself closer in his combat jacket trying to concentrate on the road ahead. But the temptation was to doze off, as the hum of the tyres lulled him towards sleep.

For a moment, Mick thought he'd seen some lights up ahead. He strained his eyes. And then he was certain. There they were, a few hundred yards in front. It looked as if it was another checkpoint. Bloody hell. Just how many were there, Mick wondered?

He jabbed Bill in the ribs and jerked him awake.

'Sorry, mate, but it's another bloody checkpoint,' Mick announced.

'What goddamn checkpoint?' Bill muttered. He rubbed the sleep from his eyes. 'We ain't had no radio call from HQ. So there ain't supposed to be no checkpoint.'

'Well take a look, mate,' said Mick. 'Looks like a checkpoint to me.'

Bill eyed the road up ahead suspiciously.

'Slow your vehicle to a crawl, buddy,' Bill said. 'Hold back as long as you can without arousing suspicion.'

Bill got on his radio and put an urgent call through to his HQ. He got an instant reply. There wasn't supposed to be a US checkpoint at this position in the road.

'I don't like this, buddy,' Bill announced. 'Get ready for fuckin' anything. See how many of 'em there are? I count a dozen, not including the ones I can't see. And they're all tooled up. I ain't sure yet. But I don't reckon this is one of ours.'

'Then who the fuck is it?' Mick asked.

'No idea, buddy,' Bill growled. 'Just be ready to put your boot on the gas.'

He eyed the checkpoint as it drew closer. 'Look, buddy. There's three different uniforms there. There's Marine Corps, there's 10th Mountain, there's even an MP. You don't never have mixed unit checkpoints. An' you see that guy out front? Holding his hand out palm towards us? That ain't the way US soldiers do a stop sign. They do a fist held forwards in the air. Always, buddy. Fist held forwards in the air.'

Bill turned to Mick. 'This ain't no US checkpoint, buddy,' Bill announced. 'It's a fuckin' ambush. We stop and we're dead. Get as close as you can. Then give her everything you got. Use the weight of the vehicle to force a way through.'

Mick nodded, keeping his eyes on the checkpoint up ahead. If Bill said it was an ambush, Mick believed him.

'Alpha One,' Mick whispered into his throat mic. 'Hostile checkpoint ahead. Prepare to run the roadblock. Follow my vehicle.'

Every man on Mick's team was on the radio net. So he knew that each soldier would have heard his warning. There was a faint grating of metal from the rear of the Land Rover. Jock and Eddie were still suffering too much to be doing much fighting. But Kiwi Jim was readying his weapons. Up front Bill had an MP5 machine-gun held between his knees. Gently as he could, he flicked the safety to off. He didn't want the lead man on the checkpoint to notice anything. Mick eased the Land Rover closer and closer to the wooden barrier. Four spotlights were flooding the area in front with light. They were blinding Mick's eyes. The soldiers up ahead were just black shapes against the white glare. But he had no doubt now that they were the enemy.

When he was just twenty yards short, Mick dropped the Land Rover into second gear. For a moment he wondered if they would make it through. Up front, Mick knew he had some serious ironwork on the vehicle. There was a massive bull bar, plus the bumper itself was like an iron girder. Mounted beneath that was a heavy winch—another hunk of solid steel. Below that again was a thick metal undershield protecting the engine. Even the headlights had solid bars over them. And the whole of the Land Rover was encased in a rollcage. It was made of heavy metal tubes the size of scaffold bars. The windscreen, the roof and the side doors were all protected in this way.

The rollcage in turn was welded to the Land Rover's solid steel chassis. With all the built-in armour plating, Mick reckoned the vehicle had to weigh at least 3 tonnes. It was powered by a 2.5 litre turbocharged diesel engine. It was weighed down by all that extra kit. But Mick knew what the vehicle was capable of. It was very highly geared. The top speed was little more than 70 m.p.h., but from 0 to 30, the power and acceleration was awesome. Mick reckoned he'd hit the checkpoint at around 30 m.p.h. Three tonnes at that speed was all but unstoppable. He thought they had a good chance to make it through.

He gritted his teeth and punched his right boot to the floor. The engine roared as the turbo cut in. They were thrown back in their seats. The enemy figure in front froze for a second, and then, at the last moment, he flung himself clear of the vehicle. As the Land Rover shot past, Bill grabbed his MP5 and pointed it out of the side window. With one hand he emptied a burst into the enemy soldier's face.

The Land Rover's bull bar splintered the wooden barrier as if it were matchwood. With its engine screaming the three tonnes of raw metal ploughed into the checkpoint. There was a deafening crash as oil drums and sandbags flew in all directions. Enemy soldiers dived for cover out of the Land Rover's path. Mick and Bill ducked as the windscreen shattered. Sheets of metal and wooden planking smashed down on the vehicle, but bounced off harmlessly, thrown clear by the steel rollcage.

For a horrible moment, Mick felt a stabbing pain in his wrists. The steering wheel had been wrenched from his grasp. He glanced up through the shattered windscreen. The front wheels had hit a pile of concrete blocks, and he fought to regain his grip as the Land Rover reared up over the jumbled blocks. Then they were climbing over the top and smashing through clear of the roadblock and back on open tarmac again.

Mick jerked the Land Rover's wheel to the right. The bull bar crushed two of the mobile spotlights as if they were tinfoil. As he pulled clear he gunned the engine and slammed it into third gear. At the same time he heard enemy rounds tearing into the rear of the Land Rover. They punched holes in the aluminium bodywork but were stopped by the armour plating.

Out of the corner of his eye Mick caught sight of a group of vehicles. Several Mercedes and a couple of Toyota jeeps were parked up by the roadside. He jerked the wheel again, this time ramming the Land Rover into the nearest Merc. There was a crunching of metal as the steel bumper ripped the front off the enemy vehicle. At the same time Kiwi Jim pounded the checkpoint with the 50-cal heavy machine-gun.

As they tore away from the wrecked Mercedes, Mick did a rapid visual check of the Toyota jeeps. If the enemy came after them, he wanted a good idea of what he was up against. The jeeps looked pretty standard and he saw no signs that they were armoured. They'd be fast on the road. But off road on tough terrain they'd be no match for the Land Rovers.

Suddenly, Mick saw Jock raising himself up in the seat behind him. He had his favourite weapon—his

GPMG—levelled at the hip. Jock must have made a miracle recovery from the Sarin gas. There was a deafening burst of gunfire as Jock opened up on the last of the enemy vehicles, pouring a concentrated burst of fire into the fuel tank of the Merc. As they accelerated away there was a massive explosion. The Merc's fuel had blown sky high.

In seconds they had shot past and hit the open road. The front of the Land Rover was covered in wreckage. Both its wing mirrors were shattered. But Mick still had a rear-view mirror in the cab. He checked behind him. To his relief he saw the two other Land Rovers powering away from the burning checkpoint. He could see the tracer flying from their heavy weapons. They were giving the enemy a serious pounding. Mick changed up into fifth gear and thrust his foot to the floor. Quickly, the wrecked checkpoint was left behind.

'Alpha One, sitrep,' Mick announced. He was asking the other vehicles to report in to him.

'Alpha Two, vehicle and team intact,' came the reply.

'Alpha Three, vehicle intact,' came Guy's voice on the net. 'But we got wounded.'

'Shit!' Mick cursed. 'How bad?'

'Couple with flesh wounds,' Guy replied. 'But I got one hit in the groin. Lot of blood. Could be his artery's hit.'

'OK. You blokes got a medic in your vehicle, right? Do what you can. Soon as possible we'll haul up so we can deal with them.'

Bollocks. The last thing they needed now was wounded. How many were there and how bad, Mick wondered? He checked his rear-view mirror, to see if he could chance stopping. But way behind he could see headlights now. They hadn't put all the enemy vehicles out of action and it looked as if they had pursuers.

'Don't this thing go no faster?' Mick asked.

'It ain't built for speed, buddy,' Bill answered. 'It's built for running enemy roadblocks. You want speed you should've taken Major Wanker's BMWs. Tell you one thing. If we had, we'd all be dead by now. They weren't expecting armoured Land Rovers. You could tell by the way they set the goddamn roadblock.'

'Well, we ain't out of the woods yet,' Mick declared. 'They're coming after us. And they're a lot fucking faster than we are.'

'So what d'you suggest, buddy?' Bill said, with a grin. 'You're the goddamn SAS. How you gonna get us outta this one?'

'Mate, this is what I suggest . . .' Mick answered.

'Alpha One,' Mick spoke into his throat mic. 'I'm looking for an ambush site. I'm stopping when I find it. Our vehicle will form the centre of the roadblock. Team Two, you take the right hand side of the road. Team Three, the left. Be ready in seconds 'cause they ain't far behind us. Keep your engines running, but kill your lights. I want to mallet the fuckers with everything we got.'

'Alpha Two, copied,' came back the reply.

'Alpha Three, copied.'

What Mick needed now was a good ambush site and fast. Up ahead was a tight bend in the road. It wasn't perfect. But it would have to do.

'Hold tight!' Mick yelled.

As he rounded the bend he slammed his foot on the brakes and wrenched the steering wheel over. In a screech of burning rubber he brought the Land Rover to a halt. It was left broadside on the road. A little later Land Rovers two and three came to a sudden halt in the dust on either side. The three vehicles formed a V-shape now, completely blocking the road. They cut their lights and the scene went totally dark. For a second Mick considered using night vision goggles for the ambush. But he quickly ruled it out. If they did so the headlights of the enemy vehicles would blind them.

Kiwi Jim and Jock swung the GPMG and the 50-cal heavy machine-guns around. Apart from the Land Rovers' engines ticking over there was silence now. Mick heard a dog barking in the distance. And then the straining of motors as the vehicles in pursuit drew nearer. Mick pulled his MP5 closer into his shoulder. He focused on the dark road behind and tensed his finger on the trigger.

'Alpha One,' Mick spoke into his mic. 'On me, open fire.'

Twenty seconds later a pair of headlights rounded the bend some 800 yards behind. The vehicle was travelling fast, 80 or 90 miles an hour. By the height of the headlights, Mick reckoned it had to be one of the Mercs. He held his fire as the vehicle raced towards him. A second and a third pair of lights appeared behind it. Suddenly there was a screeching of tyres, as the lead vehicle slammed on the brakes. The driver must have caught a glint of his lights on the Land Rovers up ahead. As the driver struggled to bring the car to a stop, Mick held his fire. He reckoned that the Merc had to be armoured. It was heavy and taking a long time to come to a halt.

Suddenly the driver lost control and the Merc spun sideways on the road. As it did so, the whole of the vehicle became visible. Instantly Mick opened fire with his MP5, raking the Merc from right to left with a barrage of fire. At the same time the big guns to either side of him let rip. The heavy 50-cal rounds tore through the Mercedes armour like a giant tin opener. There was a sharp explosion and in an instant the car became a ball of orange flame. There was a horrible screaming and Mick saw that the men inside were being burned alive. Then the hail of rounds from the Land Rovers ripped into the vehicle behind.

Back at the bend in the road Mick could see other vehicles screeching to a halt. There were a couple of Toyota jeeps and more Mercs. Figures went diving into the bushes at the side of the road, then returned fire. Quick as a flash Kiwi Jim hauled one of the light anti-armour weapons (LAWs) out of the Land Rover. In one swift movement he had the weapon armed and up on his shoulder. The Land Rover was lit up in the flash from the rocket firing. It streaked ahead in the darkness and impacted in a massive gout of flame. Bodies were thrown into the air as the two cars behind the lead Mercedes burst into flames. The whole of the road was now blocked with burning debris.

Fucking nice one, Kiwi, Mick thought. It was time to be moving again.

'Let's fuckin' MOVE!' Mick yelled.

Mick dropped his smoking weapon and gunned the engine. He wrestled the vehicle back into line and accelerated away. As he did so, Kiwi Jim and Jock kept hammering away at the enemy with the big guns. Mick put his foot to the floor and the other two Land Rovers pulled in behind him. He checked his mirror. Several of the enemy vehicles were on fire now. A tangle of burning wreckage was completely blocking the road.

'Alpha One. Keep your lights out,' Mick spoke into his mic. 'Drive on night vision only. Let's not make it easy for them to follow.'

For several minutes Mick and his team drove on in silence. He kept checking behind him. He hoped that he'd lost them. But somehow, he didn't think so. Finally, he caught a tiny pair of dots in the Land Rover's mirror. Headlights. Again they had enemy vehicles on their tail. He checked once more. As the enemy vehicles rounded a bend he counted four sets of lights. Four vehicles had got through the ambush and were still after them. He glanced across at Bill. Bill raised his eyebrows. Mick jerked a thumb behind him.

'More of the fuckers back there,' Mick said. 'They ain't giving up, mate. Not that easily.'

'We ain't gonna lose them on the road, buddy,' Bill replied. 'An' they ain't fallin' for that ambush trick again.'

'Yeah. So time to head for the desert,' said Mick. 'Ask your buddy Omar—where's the nearest point where we can leave the highway.'

Bill turned to Omar who was crammed into the back seat. They began a rushed conversation in mixed English and Arabic. Then Bill turned back to Mick.

'Two miles away, take the turn-off to the left,' Bill said. 'Omar reckons it's our best chance.'

'Alpha One. Enemy in pursuit,' Mick spoke into his radio. 'We're going to lose the road. Hit the open desert. Follow my lead. Let's see the fuckers follow us then.'

At Omar's signal, Mick took a turn onto a track to the left. Quickly, it opened out into the flat desert. Mick kept glancing in his rear-view mirror. Soon, he saw the enemy vehicles stopping at the roadside behind them. But after a short delay, he saw three sets of lights leaving the road. The vehicles turned in his direction, their headlights probing the darkness. The enemy were coming after them. It had to be the Toyota jeeps. And they must have packed them full of their men at the roadside. Still the bastards weren't giving up.

Mick jabbed Bill in the ribs. 'Tell Omar I need rough ground. Rougher the better. And tell him a river would be good. A deep one.'

Bill turned back to Omar. They spoke for a few minutes in mixed English and Bill's basic Arabic. Then Bill turned back to Mick.

'Right, buddy, how rough d'you want it?' Bill asked. 'Omar says there's a camel track coming up in about a mile. It's rougher than a Baghdad whore, or least that's how Omar put it. That do ya?'

'Sounds perfect, mate,' Mick replied. 'Let's do it. 'Cause those fuckers behind are gaining again.'

'Now that ain't all,' Bill added, grinning. 'That track that's rougher than a whore's whatsit. Well it leads to a wadi. Kinda dry riverbed. But Omar says this time of year it ain't likely to be dry. More likely to be water up to the windows. How's that suit ya?'

'Nothin' better than a wet wadi,

mate,' Mick replied.

'Of course, if it's too deep when we reach it we're trapped,' Bill added, grinning.

'Just tell me where the bloody turn-off is, mate,' Mick replied.

A minute later and Omar signalled Mick into a sidetrack. Immediately, the Land Rover started bucking and groaning, and Mick had to cut his speed. The camel track was a series of deep ruts. Even for the Land Rover it was treacherous going. After five minutes of bone-shaking progress, the track began dropping into a valley. Mick figured the riverbed would be at the valley floor. He checked his mirror. Back up behind him Mick could see the headlights of the enemy vehicles. But they had slowed to a crawl. Mick grinned to himself. It was like driving across a ploughed field, this camel track of Omar's. And nothing could beat a Land Rover across such terrain.

As they hit the valley floor, Mick caught sight of a stretch of water up ahead. It was glistening faintly in the light of the moon. He was glad he'd checked out the enemy jeeps back at the roadblock. As far as he could remember, none of them had any deep-water gear. By contrast, each of the Land Rovers was kitted out with a 'snorkel', a pipe that ran up the right-hand corner of the windscreen. It sucked in air from the height of the vehicle's roof to allow the engine to keep running under water. It meant they could drive through water to a depth of five feet or more. If the river was deep enough then the enemy were finished. Mick gunned the engine and took his vehicle to the water's edge.

'Alpha One, going wet,' Mick spoke into his radio.

It was best to warn everyone. Just so they could try to keep their weapons and ammo dry. Mick changed down into second gear, then plunged his vehicle into the water. In seconds they were in up to the level of the doors. Brown sludgy water began to pour into the cab. Mick kept the engine revving and pushed ahead. The water started streaming in through the broken windscreen. Much higher, and even they would be in trouble. He could hear the exhaust gurgling and bubbling in the river behind him. For a while the water kept rising, then the riverbed levelled off. With a surge of power, the Land Rover hauled itself up out of the water and onto the far bank. They were through!

Mick pulled over on the riverbank. His trousers were soaking wet, and his boots filled to the brim. He could hear the splashing of the river water pouring out of the cab. Checking behind him he saw the other two Land Rovers driving themselves clear of the river. They'd done it, Mick told himself. He glanced across the water. On the far side, the enemy vehicles had come to a halt. There was no way that they could follow. If they tried to they'd be finished.

'Alpha One, let's go!' Mick yelled into his radio. 'Let's get out of range. Before those fuckers try to spoil the party.'

*   *   *

Bill held out a hand to Mick. 'OK, buddy. You done it. It's mission accomplished. I got you a security escort to the airport. Then you can crack open the bubbly on the flight home.'

'*We* done it, mate,' Mick replied, as the two men shook hands. 'Without you, we'd have been toast.'

'Ah, whatever,' said Bill.

It was the day after their arrival back in Baghdad. The drive from the river crossing to the city had gone without a hitch. There had been no further sign of the enemy. Bill was still trying to find out who it was that had attacked them. He was using all his local sources to do so. But so far, there were no firm leads. Of one thing they were certain, though. It had been a well-planned ambush. The enemy had been expecting them, on that road and at that time. The only thing they hadn't been expecting was Bill's armoured Land Rovers. Bill had two good men in hospital. They'd been in the rear vehicle. Their injuries were serious, but he reckoned they'd pull through. And Bill had vowed to get his revenge.

Mick and Bill were convinced of another thing, too. The ambush had been meant to take them alive. To capture them, or something, without damaging the painting. Normally, they would have slowed to a stop at a US military checkpoint. If they'd done so at this one, weapons would have been stuck in their faces. They would have been hauled out of the vehicles at gunpoint. And what would have happened next didn't bear thinking about. Bill was certain that whoever had set the ambush was after one thing. The painting. Which meant that someone, somewhere had betrayed them.

'I'll be seeing you, buddy,' Bill remarked. 'It's just until the next time. An' there is gonna be a next time, isn't there? There'd better be. I enjoyed this one too much for it to be the last.'

'Sure thing, mate,' Mick replied. 'Maybe I need to jack in that photography job. Pay's shit. Come out here'n work with you?'

'Any time, buddy. I'd kill for guys like you on my team. Any of you. You're always welcome. So long, buddy. Take real good care of that painting now, won't ya?'

'Cheers, mate. East End Eddie there's got it. And there's no one going to take it off him in a hurry.'

With that, Mick turned and jumped in his vehicle for the short drive to the airport.

CHAPTER NINE

The four men stood in line at the BA check-in desk. They weren't overly nervous. As Bill had said, it was mission accomplished. Time to relax and enjoy the flight home. Eddie still had his bandages. And Jock was wheezing from the effects of the Sarin. But it could have been a lot worse for either of them. They looked little different from the other private military operators passing through Iraq's main airport. Back at Bill's villa Eddie had sewn the painting into the lining of his jacket. Just like Tony, his dodgy art thief mate, had told him to. What could go wrong now?

Then, as the men chatted away, an Iraqi airport guard came up to them.

'Excuse me, sirs,' the Iraqi began politely. 'I just have few questions for you, sirs.'

'Sure,' Mick replied. 'Fire away, mate.'

'If you please follow me?' said the Iraqi. 'It will only take one moment.'

The four men looked at each other. Maybe it was just routine questioning? In any case, they had little choice but to do as the Iraqi asked. The airport was bristling with armed security guards. Silently, they followed him off to a side room. As soon as they were inside the door, Mick froze. He couldn't believe his eyes. There in the centre of the room was the unmistakable figure of 'Major Wanker'. He was flanked on either side by several Iraqi security guards.

'What the fuck?!' Mick blurted out.

'Gentlemen,' the Major began, smiling broadly. 'So nice to see you all again. Congratulations. A successful mission, I hear.'

'What the hell are you doing here?' Mick replied.

'Simple. A change of plan, Mick,' the Major replied. 'The Kuwaiti prince is so pleased he wants the painting flown direct to Kuwait. That's why I'm here. To meet his request. Everyone is very pleased. You have all done very well. You'll be rewarded accordingly.'

'Why didn't you come and meet us at Bill's villa, Major?' Mick asked. 'Why pull this little stunt at the airport?'

'What stunt, Mick?' the Major beamed. 'Plans change all the time. Surely you know that. Being ex-SAS and all that. So, which one of you has the painting?'

The Major's eyes darted around the four men. No one answered.

' 'Old on one effing minute,' Eddie said. 'Why ain't we invited to deliver it in person to his Royal Highness? We just risked our necks rescuing it, didn't we?'

'Good idea. We'll come with you, Major,' Mick added. 'You'll be needing a security escort on the journey. Don't want the painting going missing again, do we?'

'Stop playing silly buggers,' the Major snapped. 'You're not invited. And if you hadn't noticed, I have my own security with me.' The Major nodded at the Iraqi guards on either side of him. 'Now, I'm not messing around. Hand over the painting.'

Mick glanced around the room. They clearly had no option. There were half a dozen Iraqi guards. Each had an AK47 assault rifle pointed in their direction.

'Best you do as the fucker says,' Mick growled.

''Ave a load of this, then,' said Eddie. He slipped off his combat jacket and tossed it to the Major.

'It's the damn painting I'm after,' the Major snarled. 'What the hell do I want with this stinking rag?'

'Take it easy,' Eddie replied. 'No need to be like that. You got the effing painting. It's sewn into the lining of me jacket.'

'What?!' the Major yelled. He stared at the combat jacket. 'You stupid idiot. You better not have damaged it, let me tell you.'

'Getting a bit worked up, aren't you, mate?' Kiwi Jim said. 'Over a worthless painting and all?'

'Just take it easy,' Eddie added. 'I may not talk posh but I ain't totally effing stupid. It's in there and it's safe as houses. Take a look.'

The Major snapped his fingers and muttered a command in Arabic. One of the Iraqi guards produced a knife. Carefully, the Major inserted the blade into the jacket. He cut open a section of the lining, revealing one corner of the canvas. It was sewn neatly into the jacket, the stitches only touching the outer edges. The Major looked up from the jacket and broke into a broad smile.

'That's better,' he purred. 'Now we can all be friends again. You men have a plane to catch, I believe. As do I. Once the prince has his painting, you'll get the rest of your money. So, no hard feelings, eh? I think it's time we all were on our way.'

'We'll be seeing you, Major,' Mick replied icily.

'Not if I see you first,' said the Major, as he turned to leave.

'Just you take care of that Van Gogh now,' Eddie called after him. 'Wouldn't want to see it going missing again, would we?'

The Major froze in his tracks. He turned to face Eddie. His face had drained of all its colour. And Mick, Kiwi Jim and Jock were all staring at Eddie in surprise.

'What did you say?' the Major snarled.

'I'm a bit of an art buff, see,' Eddie replied. 'I reckon that's Vincent's work, if ever I effing saw it. Worth a tidy packet it is, an' all.'

'Is it?' the Major sneered. 'Well, let me tell you something. You're no art buff, Eddie. You're a sorry, has-been soldier. You were the best once. But you're a hired killer these days. Doing the dirty work for others.'

'Yeah, and you're full of shit, mate,' Eddie replied. 'Never was no Government mission, was there? Nor no effing prince, neither. It was a private operation all along, wasn't it, Major? Painting's worth a mint, ain't it? Most of Vincent's stuff is, so I'm told.'

'Is that so?' the Major replied. 'Thinking of changing careers, are we, Eddie? From hired gun to art expert in one easy step, is that it? Somehow, I don't think so. Stick to killing, Eddie. It's the only thing you do even half well.'

'It was all to benefit your effing bank account, wasn't it, Major?' said Eddie. 'You got the painting, mate. That's what you wanted. You can admit it now, can't you?'

'You'd better watch what you say,' said the Major, smiling coldly.

'Making accusations like that could land you in a lot of trouble.'

'No worries, mate,' Kiwi cut in. 'You're a dead man already. Wherever you go. Wherever you hide. I'll still find you.'

'Don't threaten me,' the Major shot back. 'With a painting like this, I'm rich enough to afford the best. The best security money can buy. Maybe I'd even have considered using your services once. But not now. Now it's goodbye. Goodbye and thanks, gentlemen. You've done an excellent job.'

'So, it's bloody true?' Mick gasped. 'You bastard—'

'Of course it's true,' said the Major, bursting into laughter. 'It's all true. Are you really only starting to grasp that now, Mick? Seems the only one of you wise enough to realise it was Eddie. And he's hardly Einstein, is he?'

'So who the fuck paid?' Mick growled. 'The hundred and fifty grand was in our accounts. I checked—'

'I did, Mickey,' the Major replied. 'I paid. Or rather, the Lloyd-Barrier family money did. Two million dollars invested. For a priceless Van Gogh. Quite a good return, wouldn't you agree? Or a nice little earner, as you gentlemen might say.'

'We just gassed a load of Iraqis,' Mick spat out. 'Wiped 'em out. All so you could get your hands on that painting. On the money. You dirty, murdering bastard.'

'You watch your mouth,' the Major snapped. 'Poor bleeding heart. Feel sorry for them, do you? They were low life. Scum. Iraq and the world is a better place without them.'

The Major turned to one of the guards. He barked a few orders at him in Arabic. The guard turned back to Mick and his team with cold eyes.

'The guards have orders to hold you here until I'm long gone,' said the Major. 'So don't try anything stupid. And just remember. You have all been involved in an illegal operation. You just murdered a bunch of petty thieves using Sarin gas. That is a very serious crime. You breathe a word of this to anyone and we all go down. We're all in this together, now. So, I'd stay quiet if I were you. Dead quiet. For a very long time.'

The Major turned and headed for the rear exit.

'Just one more thing, Major,' Mick called after him. 'Why didn't you level with us? You could have told us from the start it was a private job. Why the need to double-cross us?'

'Because you wouldn't have done it, that's why,' the Major replied. 'You needed to believe it was for Queen and Country, as well as the money. You still believe in loyalty, Mick. Decency. Patriotism. Honour. Maybe one day you'll wise up. It's every man for himself, Mick. Always has been. Always will be. Honest, decent people like you don't get ahead.'

'You're wrong,' Mick replied. 'We'd have done it just for the cash.'

He was lying. But he was trying to provoke the Major. Trying to get him to reveal as much of the truth as possible. The more Mick could find out now, the easier it would be to hunt the Major down. For there was no doubt in Mick's mind. Even if it took him the rest of his life. He was going to track that bastard down and get his revenge.

'Would you?' the Major sneered. 'Just for the money, eh? And how would that have worked, I wonder? I would have told you the truth, would I? That the painting was worth forty million dollars. And then I would have trusted you to go get it for me. Is that it? D'you really think I'm that stupid?'

'It was you who set the ambush for us, wasn't it, Major?' said Mick. His voice was like murder now. 'You set the ambush. So there would be no witnesses. And to save paying us the rest of the money.'

'What ambush?' the Major replied, smiling. 'What money? Iraq's a very dangerous place, Mick. You should know that by now. You should thank your lucky stars you got out alive. I should be careful from now on. Best you behave. Never know who might be after you. Bye-bye, gentlemen. It's been a wonderful adventure. But now it's over. And time I was leaving you.'

'Let the fucker go, Mickey,' Eddie said, placing a hand on Mick's arm. 'He ain't worth the grief. Let 'im go.'

CHAPTER TEN

Mick slammed the Land Rover into reverse and spun her out of the parking space. Two weeks parked at

Heathrow Airport had cost him a fortune, as always. He gunned the engine and headed for the exit. Needless to say, none of the lads had spoken much on the flight home. They'd been exhausted. They'd slept most of the journey.

'Right, now the real fucking mission begins,' Mick snarled. He pulled out onto the tarmac road. 'Tracking down Major fucking Wanker. I want that bastard real bad.'

'Not as much as me, mate,' Kiwi added.

'Why effing bother?' said Eddie. 'He's a tosser. Who'd want to spend time in his company?'

'If I was torturing him with a hot iron—that'd be all right,' Kiwi cut in.

'Nah. Fuck 'im,' Eddie replied, laughing. 'Forget it. Life's all right. Never been better, if you ask me.'

'What the hell is it with you?' Mick snapped. 'We've all just been buggered big time. And you're sounding positively fucking joyful. You cracked up or something?'

'Not me, mate,' Eddie replied, with a grin. 'I got every reason to be a very happy boy, I 'ave.'

'Like fucking what?' Mick snapped.

'Like pass me me bag, Kiwi,' Eddie said. 'That's it. That one. Pass it over 'ere. Now, what do we 'ave in 'ere? Me Paraclete body armour, that's what we 'ave. Best body armour money can buy. Cor blimey, heavy, ain't it? Pity to have to ruin it.'

'Will you shut the fuck up, Eddie,' said Mick, skidding to a halt on the roadside. 'Or d'you want out of the Land Rover and fucking walking home?'

'Whatever, mate,' Eddie replied. He pulled a knife out of his bag. 'But I don't reckon you'd want to miss this little show. Not for the world, mate.'

'What bloody show?' Mick snapped.

'Patience, dear boy,' Eddie replied, in a mock posh accent. 'Patience.'

He began slicing open the lining of his body armour. As he did so he whistled a jolly tune to himself. Mick was about to smack him, he was getting so angry. But he also had to see what the crazy bastard was up to now. Mick watched the blade slicing through the tough material. Suddenly, he caught sight of the corner of something sticking out from the green lining. For a second, Mick couldn't believe his eyes. Eddie carried on whistling, and slicing away at the lining. Soon the bottom edge of a sheet of canvas was visible.

'What the fuck?' said Mick. 'It can't be!'

'Can't be what, mate?' Eddie replied. 'Van Gogh's *Vase with Irises Against a Yellow Background*? Well it is if I'm not mistaken. And an original it is, too, old boy.'

'But you handed Major Wanker the bloody painting,' Mick blurted out. 'Back in Baghdad. I saw it. I saw you do it. I saw him check it. Then leave the room.'

'Indeed I did,' Eddie replied. 'But did Major Wanker check that it was an original Van Gogh? No he didn't, did he?'

'You crafty fucker . . .' Mick began. 'That dodgy art thief mate of yours? You cooked up some deal with him, didn't you?'

'At this moment Major effing Wanker is in possession of a painting,' Eddie announced. 'A picture of a vase of flowers. It's signed "Vincent". But the real painter is Timmy Brown. A mate of a mate of mine and the best forger in all London town.'

'You bastard!' Mick yelled, grabbing Eddie's head in an armlock. 'You lovely, lovely fuckin' bastard. And you didn't bloody tell us one word about it, did you? I'm going to murder you.'

The four men in the Land Rover

burst into wild cheering. They hugged and punched each other. They couldn't believe it. East End Eddie had got the better of Major Lloyd-Barrier, the world's biggest bastard. And they'd got their hands on a 45-million dollar painting.

Just at that moment, a police car drew up beside Mick's Land Rover. A uniformed officer approached the vehicle's passenger door. There was a tap on the window. Just as Eddie went to wind it down, Mick stopped him.

'Hide the bloody painting first, mate,' said Mick.

'What?' Eddie said. 'It's just effing Billy blue hat, mate. What you worried about?'

'Maybe the fucking Major's reported us,' said Mick. 'Dobbed us in to the coppers.'

'You hide it, then, mate,' Eddie said. He handed Mick the body armour and wound down the window.

'Excuse me, lads,' the officer said. 'But you're parked in a restricted area. This is Heathrow Airport. Can I see some ID?'

'Officer, let me let you into a little secret,' Eddie announced. 'We're on a secret mission. Just back from Baghdad. Having a little celebration, that's all. Here's me badge.'

Eddie fished around in his bag and pulled out his beige SAS beret. He still carried it on all his missions. He flashed the officer his SAS cap badge.

'I got the code word if you want it, mate,' Eddie added. 'You know, the little secret word that lets us go on our way.'

'You boys SAS?' the officer asked. He seemed a little in awe of them now. 'Erm, sorry to have troubled you, lads. Good luck with whatever mission you're on. But I guess if you're SAS you won't be needing too much luck, will you?'

'Who dares, wins,' Eddie replied.

'You got it. But don't worry, mate. It's mission accomplished already. We're on our way home. Wouldn't you say so, lads?'

GLOSSARY:

50-cal—common name for the .50 calibre Browning heavy machine-gun

AK47—Soviet bloc assault rifle

Atropine—nerve agent antidote

Delta Force—US military elite special forces unit

Desert Claw—name of the mission to seize Van Gogh painting

Eagle Claw—name of the 1980 abortive US mission to rescue American hostage held in Iran

Geneva Convention—international treaty governing the rules of war

GPMG—General Purpose Machine Gun, heavy machine-gun popular with UK and US military

GPS—global positioning system

HMG—Her Majesty's Government

HQ—headquarters

LAW—light anti-armour weapon, a hand held rocket launcher used by

British and US military

M16—main type of assault rifle in use with US military forces

MP—military police

MP5—Heckler & Koch sub-machine-gun popular with elite special forces units

NAPS—Nerve Agent Pre-treatment Set, drugs used to protect against chemical and biological weapons

Sarin—a type of nerve gas developed by the German military during World War Two

SAS—Special Air Service, Britain's foremost elite special forces unit

SBS—Special Boat Service, sister special forces regiment to the SAS

SCUD—medium range missiles of Soviet origin used by Iraqi military under Saddam

SEAL—Sea Air Land, US military elite special forces and sister unit to Delta Force

SIG-Sauer—Swiss weapons manu-facturer whose pistol is popular with UK special forces

WMD—weapons of mass destruction